reasons men love unrealistic women

GUIDES MADE EASY FOR A WOMAN IN A RELATIONSHIP

Peter Eikhuemelo

ISBN 978-93-5883-039-2

Published in India 2023 by Pencil

A brand of
One Point Six Technologies Pvt. Ltd.
Unit no. 26, Ground Floor, Building A1,
Wadala Truck Terminal Road,
Near Post Office, Antop Hill, Mumbai - 400037
E connect@thepencilapp.com
W www.thepencilapp.com

Author biography

Peter Eikhuemelo is an accomplished writer known for their captivating storytelling and thought-provoking narratives. With a passion for exploring the complexities of human relationships and societal dynamics, He has crafted a diverse body of work that encompasses various genres, including fiction, romance, and contemporary literature. Their ability to create compelling characters and delve into the depths of human emotions has garnered critical acclaim and a loyal readership. Drawing inspiration from personal experiences, cultural observations, and a keen understanding of human nature, He weaves intricate tales that resonate with readers worldwide. Their works offer profound insights, challenging readers to question societal norms, explore the intricacies of love and identity, and contemplate the human condition. Through their evocative prose and ability to capture the essence of the human experience, He continues to leave a lasting impact on the literary world.

CONTENTS

Introduction

Once upon a time, in an old-fashioned little town, lived a female named Lily. She was kind-hearted, gentle, and always put others before herself. However, when it came to relationships, she often found herself feeling unfulfilled and taken for granted. One day, Lily stumbled upon an ancient book titled The Relationship Guide to Nice Women. Intrigued, she delved into its pages, discovering valuable lessons. It taught her the importance of setting boundaries, expressing her needs, and valuing her own worth. Armed with newfound knowledge, Lily embarked on a journey of self-discovery. She learned to love herself unconditionally and embraced her own desires. By communicating honestly and openly, she attracted people who cherished her kind nature and reciprocated her kindness. With time, Lily's life blossomed with meaningful connections and true love. She realized that being a nice woman didn't mean sacrificing her own happiness. Instead, it meant finding balance and embracing her own strength. From that day forward, Lily became a living example, guiding other nice women on their path to self-empowerment and fulfilling relationships. Together, they transformed their lives and inspired others to embrace their authenticity, proving that being nice doesn't have to come at the cost of their own happiness.

DORMANT TO DREAMGIRL INSTEAD

Meeting A Nice Girl

He walked into a bustling café on a sunny Saturday afternoon, the enticing aroma of freshly brewed coffee filling the air. As he scanned the room for an empty table, his eyes locked with a warm, inviting gaze. It was her—a girl with a radiant smile that seemed to brighten the entire room. His heart skipped a beat, and he couldn't resist but approach her. With a nervous yet determined stride, he mustered the courage to introduce himself. Their verbal exchange flowed effortlessly, as though they'd regarded every different for years. They discovered shared interests, exchanged witty banter, and laughed together, the sound of their joy harmonizing with the café's gentle hum. Hours passed unnoticed lost in their captivating connection. They spoke of their dreams, aspirations, and the adventures they longed to embark upon. The world outside seemed to fade away as they delved deeper into their thoughts, discovering a profound understanding of one another. Days became weeks, and their bond handiest grew stronger. They explored the city together, discovering hidden gems and creating memories. Their hearts danced in sync, their spirits entwined, as they uncovered each other's quirks, vulnerabilities, and strengths. They supported each other's passions and celebrated every milestone, nurturing a sense of shared purpose. Their relationship became a sanctuary—a space where they could be unapologetically themselves. They reveled in both the ordinary and extraordinary moments, finding solace in the comforting presence of the other. They navigated life's challenges hand in hand, offering unwavering support, and finding strength in their unity. As time passed, their love deepened, blossoming into something extraordinary. They discovered the profound beauty of vulnerability, trust, and unconditional acceptance. Their connection transcended the surface, reaching depths they had never thought possible. Together, they embarked on an incredible journey of growth, constantly pushing each other to be the best versions of themselves. In each other's embrace, they found solace and security, knowing that their hearts had found their rightful place. They nurtured their love with tenderness and compassion, savoring every stolen kiss, every shared laugh, and every stolen glance. Their relationship was a sanctuary—a refuge from the chaos of the world, where they could find solace in each other's arms. And so, their love story continues to unfold, as they traverse the unpredictable path of life hand in hand. United by their shared experiences and a love that knows no bounds, they cherish every moment, grateful for the serendipitous encounter that brought them together.

WHY DO MEN LOVE UNREALISTIC WOMEN

CRACKING THE CODE

In the vibrant city of Willow Brook, there lived a young man named Lucas. He was a charming and ambitious individual, known for his magnetic personality and captivating smile. However, beneath his confident exterior, Lucas carried a secret desire—one that puzzled both himself and those who knew him well. He found himself inexplicably drawn to women who embodied unrealistic ideals of beauty and perfection.

Lucas's fascination with these idealized women stemmed from a variety of sources. From a young age, he was bombarded with carefully curated images in magazines, billboards, and movies, portraying women with flawless features, slender figures, and unattainable beauty. These standards of perfection seeped into his subconscious, subtly shaping his preferences as he grew older.

As Lucas began to explore romantic relationships, he found himself gravitating toward women who aligned with these impossible ideals. He yearned for a partner who possessed physical attributes that matched the images he had ingrained in his mind. He couldn't help but be captivated by the idea of a woman who seemed flawless, both inside and out.

The media played a significant role in perpetuating these unrealistic expectations. Advertisements showcased women as objects of desire, often promoting a narrow definition of beauty that was unattainable for the majority. Lucas, like many others, fell into the trap of believing that such women represented the epitome of desirability and success.

But as Lucas delved deeper into his pursuit of perfection, he started to realize the inherent flaws in his approach. He discovered that his preference for unrealistic women was rooted in a mix of societal conditioning, insecurity, and the fear of settling for less. He began to question the authenticity and sustainability of his choices, recognizing that true beauty lies in embracing individuality and imperfections.

One fateful evening, Lucas attended a social gathering where he met Sarah—a vibrant, confident woman who defied societal expectations. Sarah possessed a radiance that emanated from her self-assured nature, and her genuine warmth drew Lucas in. Despite not conforming to the conventional beauty standards he had once fixated on, Lucas found himself inexplicably attracted to Sarah's authenticity and inner beauty.

One fateful evening, Lucas attended a social gathering where he met Sarah—a vibrant, confident woman who defied societal expectations. Sarah possessed a radiance that emanated from her self-assured nature, and her genuine warmth drew Lucas in. Despite not conforming to the conventional beauty standards he had once fixated on, Lucas found himself inexplicably attracted to Sarah's authenticity and inner beauty.

As Lucas spent time getting to know Sarah, he realized that his obsession with unrealistic women had hindered his ability to form meaningful connections in the past. Sarah's uniqueness challenged his preconceived notions, teaching him to appreciate the richness of diversity and the beauty that exists beyond physical appearances.

Inspired by his transformative encounter with Sarah, Lucas embarked on a journey of self-reflection and personal growth. He sought to dismantle the societal pressures that had influenced his preferences, realizing that the media's portrayal of beauty was a distorted fantasy. He became an advocate for embracing diverse forms of beauty and celebrating individuality.

Lucas's newfound perspective influenced his approach to relationships. He learned to value qualities such as kindness, intelligence, and emotional compatibility over superficial appearances. He understood that unrealistic beauty standards only perpetuated insecurities and hindered the potential for genuine connections.

As Lucas shared his insights with others, he became a catalyst for change. Through conversations and his own example, he encouraged men and women alike to question the unrealistic expectations society imposed upon them. He urged them to seek relationships based on authenticity, compassion, and shared values, rather than an unattainable fantasy.

Over time, Lucas's journey and message resonated with countless individuals who had also fallen prey to society's notion of perfection. Together, they began to redefine beauty, embracing their unique attributes and encouraging others to do the same.

In the end, Lucas discovered that his preference for unrealistic women stemmed from a combination of societal influence and personal insecurities. Through self-reflection, he realized that true happiness and fulfillment lie in accepting and celebrating the beauty that exists in reality—the beauty that transcends narrow standards

CRAZY LIKE AN ENEMY

HOW CAN YOU PERSUADE HIM THAT HE IS IN CHARGE WHILE YOU RUN THE SHOW

In the bustling city of Luminaire, there lived a young man named Alex. Alex was known for his ambitious nature and strong-willed personality. He prided himself on being in control of every aspect of his life, from his career to his relationships. Little did he know that an encounter with a captivating woman named Olivia would turn his world upside down.

Olivia was a free-spirited and intelligent woman, who radiated confidence and charisma. She had a way of captivating those around her, effortlessly drawing them into her magnetic charm. From the moment Alex laid eyes on her at a mutual friend's gathering, he felt an unexplainable connection—a sense of intrigue that he had never experienced before.

As Alex and Olivia began spending more time together, it became evident that she possessed an uncanny ability to influence him while maintaining an illusion of his control. Olivia seemed to anticipate Alex's desires and needs even before he voiced them. She effortlessly steered conversations, subtly guiding them toward her desired outcomes. It was as if she held the strings, while Alex believed he was the puppeteer.

Curiosity piqued, Alex found himself questioning the dynamics of their relationship. He wondered how Olivia managed to maintain an illusion of his control while skillfully maneuvering their interactions. Was she intentionally manipulating him, or was there something more at play?

One evening, as they strolled through the vibrant city streets, Alex decided to broach the subject. He approached Olivia with an open mind, seeking to understand the intricacies of their connection. To his surprise, Olivia welcomed the conversation with a warm smile, demonstrating her confidence and transparency.

She explained that her ability to subtly guide their interactions stemmed from her deep understanding of Alex's preferences and desires. Olivia had observed his behaviors, listened attentively to his words, and honed her intuition to anticipate his needs. She never sought to control him but rather aimed to create an environment where their desires aligned seamlessly.

As they delved deeper into their conversation, Olivia revealed that her intention was to create a partnership built on trust and mutual growth. She emphasized the importance of communication, encouraging Alex to voice his thoughts and desires openly. Olivia believed that true power lay not in dominating another person, but in fostering a sense of equality and collaboration.

As their relationship blossomed, Alex began to appreciate the beauty of their dynamic. He realized that Olivia's influence wasn't about manipulation, but rather a testament to her deep understanding of him as an individual. Her ability to create an atmosphere where their desires harmonized allowed them to navigate life together as a cohesive unit.

With Olivia's guidance, Alex learned to relinquish the need for absolute control. He discovered the strength in vulnerability, as he confided in Olivia and allowed her to support him through life's challenges. He came to understand that being in control didn't mean he had to carry the weight of the world alone—it meant trusting in the partnership they had cultivated.

Together, they embarked on a journey of self-discovery, pushing each other to reach new heights while nurturing their individual passions. Alex marveled at Olivia's unwavering support, as she celebrated his achievements and gently nudged him towards his goals.

In time, Alex realized that Olivia's influence was not about overpowering him, but about empowering him. She recognized his potential and provided the gentle guidance and encouragement he needed to flourish. Their relationship became a harmonious dance, where both partners contributed their unique strengths to create a life that exceeded their individual dreams.

As they continued to traverse life's joys and challenges, Alex and Olivia inspired those around them with their deep connection and shared vision. They showed the world that true strength and fulfillment could be found in a relationship where both partners, while seemingly in control, worked together to create a life full of love, trust, and endless possibilities.

LEAPING OVER HOOPS

WHEN WOMEN GIVE UP CONTROL AND BEC OME DEPENDENT

In a land nestled amidst rolling hills and blooming meadows, there lived a younger female named Elena. Blessed with grace and beauty, she possessed a heart as vast as the endless sky. Elena had a magnetic charm that drew people towards her, but little did she know that her own nature would lead her on a journey of self-discovery. Elena's story began when she met a charming suitor named Sebastian. His charisma and eloquence swept her off her feet, igniting a spark that promised a future filled with love and happiness. With each passing day, Elena found herself entwined in a whirlwind romance, eagerly showering Sebastian with affection and attention. In her fervent desire to please him, Elena gradually began to lose herself. She placed her own needs and aspirations on the backburner, devoting her time and energy solely to Sebastian's happiness. She became a reflection of his desires, molding herself to fit into his world, all the while neglecting her own dreams and aspirations. Unbeknownst to Elena, this self-sacrifice gradually transformed her into a woman in need. She sought constant reassurance and validation, desperately craving Sebastian's attention and approval. Her once confident spirit was overshadowed by insecurity, and her independence gave way to dependency.

As time passed, Sebastian became overwhelmed by Elena's neediness. The vibrant, self-assured woman he fell in love with had become a shadow of her former self. He yearned for the woman who had captured his heart, not the dependent soul she had become. This realization prompted Sebastian to address their relationship, urging Elena to rediscover her own identity and reclaim her independence.

Heartbroken yet determined, Elena embarked on a journey of self-reflection and growth. She realized that her neediness stemmed from a lack of self-love and self-acceptance. As she explored the depths of her own soul, she discovered that true happiness could only be found by embracing her own passions, dreams, and desires.

Elena slowly unraveled the layers of dependency that had entangled her, learning to love and nurture herself. She sought solace in her own company and discovered the joy of pursuing her own interests. With time, her radiance returned, shining brighter than ever before.

As Elena reclaimed her independence, her path crossed with that of a kind-hearted artist named Lucas. Their connection was rooted in mutual respect, support, and admiration. Lucas celebrated Elena's strength and encouraged her to pursue her dreams, while she, in turn, embraced his artistic endeavors with genuine interest and love.

Together, Elena and Lucas embarked on a journey of love and growth, nurturing each other's individuality while fostering a strong and interdependent bond. They understood the importance of maintaining their own identities and dreams, while cherishing the shared moments that brought them closer.

In this tale, the focus is not solely on women giving themselves away and becoming needy, but rather on the transformative power of self-love and reclaiming one's independence. Elena's story serves as a reminder that true happiness lies in embracing our own individuality, nurturing our dreams, and finding balance in our relationships.

CONFECTION STORE

HOW TO MAXIMIZE YOUR FEMININE AND SEXUAL ABILITIES

In a land of timeless beauty and abundant wisdom, there dwelled a young woman named Seraphina. Radiant and alluring, she possessed an innate understanding of the immense power contained within her femininity and sexuality. Seraphina's journey to harness and embrace these powers was one of self-discovery, empowerment, and profound enlightenment.

Seraphina began her quest by delving deep into her own essence, seeking to understand the intricate tapestry of her desires, dreams, and passions. She recognized that true power lay not in conforming to societal expectations or norms but in embracing her authenticity and unique expression of womanhood.

With a thirst for knowledge, Seraphina sought out ancient teachings from wise women who had come before her. She learned the secrets of sacred femininity and the sacredness of her body. She discovered that her sensuality was not to be feared or suppressed but celebrated and honored as a divine gift.

Through the art of self-care, Seraphina nurtured her body, mind, and spirit. She cultivated a deep connection with herself, practicing mindfulness and self-love. Seraphina understood that when she treated herself with kindness and compassion, her feminine and sexual powers blossomed like a magnificent flower, radiating beauty and allure.

In her interactions with others, Seraphina embraced her inherent magnetism, understanding that her presence had the potential to uplift and inspire. She embraced the power of her voice, speaking her truth with confidence and grace. Seraphina discovered that by nurturing authentic connections and creating spaces of love and acceptance, she could influence others positively, fostering a ripple effect of empowerment.

But Seraphina's journey was not without challenges. She faced moments of doubt and societal pressures that sought to diminish her power. In those moments, she turned inward, drawing strength from the depths of her being. She reminded herself of her inherent worth and the divine spark that resided within her.

Seraphina discovered the importance of boundaries, understanding that her power required protection. She learned to say no when necessary and to honor her own needs and desires. By cultivating healthy boundaries, she created a sanctuary for her feminine and sexual powers to flourish, unburdened by external expectations.

As Seraphina grew in her understanding and embodiment of her femininity and sexuality, she realized that her power was not solely for personal gain but for the greater good. She used her influence to advocate for equality, justice, and the upliftment of all women. Seraphina recognized that by empowering others, she expanded the collective power of femininity, creating a world that honored and respected the inherent strength within every woman.

In the end, Seraphina's journey was not just about embracing her feminine and sexual powers but also about embracing her true essence. She understood that her power stemmed from a deep connection with herself and the unwavering belief in her own worth. Seraphina's story became an eternal inspiration, reminding women across generations to embrace their femininity, honor their sexuality, and unleash the limitless power that lies within.

NO MORE NAGGING

WHAT TO DO IF SHE IS TAKEN FOR GRANTED AND WHEN TO ACT

In the magnificent kingdom of Veridonia, there lived a young woman named Amara. She possessed a heart as pure as the crystal-clear springs that flowed through the land. Amara's beauty radiated from within, captivating all who had the pleasure of knowing her.

Amara's path took a tumultuous turn when she fell deeply in love with a man named Lucas. In the beginning, their love was a tapestry woven with joy and tenderness. But as time passed, Lucas began to take Amara's love for granted, oblivious to the depth of her affection and the effort she put into their relationship.

Heartache began to cloud Amara's once bright spirit. She yearned for the days when Lucas cherished her every word and appreciated her presence. Determined to find a way to mend their connection, Amara sought counsel from the wise women of Veridonia.

The wise women, known for their ancient wisdom, shared their insights with Amara. They explained that when someone takes you for granted, it is essential to first recognize and honor your own worth. They advised her to cultivate self-love and self-respect, for only then could she demand the same from others.

Armed with this wisdom, Amara embarked on a journey of self-discovery. She dedicated time to nourish her passions and pursue her dreams. Through self-reflection, she unearthed her unique strengths and talents, building her confidence and reminding herself of the incredible woman she was.

Next, the wise women guided Amara in open and honest communication. They encouraged her to express her feelings to Lucas, sharing how his actions made her feel undervalued and unappreciated. With their guidance, Amara learned to communicate her needs assertively, seeking understanding and empathy from her beloved.

Though Lucas initially seemed unresponsive to Amara's heartfelt plea, she remained steadfast in her determination to restore their love. The wise women advised her to set healthy boundaries, showing Lucas that she would not tolerate being taken for granted any longer. Amara lovingly communicated her boundaries, making it clear that her love was a gift to be cherished, not a possession to be taken lightly.

As time passed, Lucas began to notice the transformation in Amara. He witnessed her blossoming confidence and the radiance that emanated from her soul. Her pursuit of personal growth and the establishment of boundaries awakened him to the depth of his actions and the treasure he had been neglecting.

Realizing the gravity of his mistake, Lucas approached Amara with humility and remorse. He expressed his regret for taking her for granted and vowed to change his ways, recognizing the immeasurable value of her love and presence in his life.

Amara, though initially guarded, saw the sincerity in Lucas' eyes. She understood that his transformation required patience and forgiveness. Guided by her own growth and the wisdom of the wise women, Amara chose to grant him a second chance, with the understanding that their love would be built on mutual respect and appreciation.

Together, Amara and Lucas embarked on a new chapter of their love story, one rooted in gratitude and a deepened understanding of the importance of cherishing and valuing each other. Through the challenges they faced and the lessons learned, their bond grew stronger and more resilient, becoming a testament to the transformative power of love and the strength found in overcoming adversity.

In the kingdom of Veridonia, the tale of Amara and Lucas served as a reminder to all that love requires constant nourishment, appreciation, and a willingness to grow together. It taught the people of the land to never settle for being taken for granted and to always uphold the value of their own worth. And so, their story became an eternal inspiration, illuminating the path towards a love that endures and flourishes in the face

THE CONFIDENTIAL PLAYBOOK OF THE OTHER GROUP

THINGS HE ALLEGEDLY SAID THAT YOU NEVER HEARD HIM SAY

In a distant land veiled by mist and mystery, there lived a solitary figure known as the Whisperer. Clad in a cloak of shadows, he traversed the realms, his enigmatic presence arousing curiosity among those who caught a glimpse of him. The townspeople suspected that the Whisperer held secrets that could unravel the very fabric of their reality, but they had never heard him utter a single word.

As the years passed, rumors began to circulate about the Whisperer's origins. Some whispered that he had once been a sorcerer of great power, capable of wielding magic that defied comprehension. Others suspected that he possessed the wisdom of ancient sages, having delved deep into the forgotten tombs of knowledge. Yet, amidst the whispers and conjectures, the true nature of the Whisperer remained veiled in ambiguity.

In the heart of the village, a young woman named Elara nurtured an unspoken fascination with the enigmatic figure. Her curious eyes were drawn to the way he observed the world, as if seeing beyond the surface of reality. Elara suspected that the Whisperer possessed a connection to the ethereal realm, a link to the unseen spirits that danced in the moonlit shadows. However, she had never heard him express his intimate connection with the otherworldly forces that guided his every step.

Across the bustling town square, a humble blacksmith named Roland caught glimpses of the Whisperer from his workshop. As the sparks from his anvil illuminated the darkness, Roland couldn't help but suspect that the enigmatic figure harbored an unparalleled mastery of swordplay. The grace with which the Whisperer moved, evading the invisible strikes of the wind itself, hinted at a hidden expertise in the ancient art of combat. Yet, Roland had never heard the Whisperer speak of his exceptional martial skills.

In the depths of the neighboring forest, a wise herbalist named Lillian gathered herbs and plants imbued with potent medicinal properties. Lillian had long suspected that the Whisperer possessed an intimate bond with nature, a communion with the ancient spirits that whispered through the leaves and danced upon the ripples of the nearby stream. The way he walked with reverence, leaving naught but a whisper in his wake, suggested a deep connection to the natural world. Yet, Lillian had never heard the Whisperer share his profound affinity for the realm of flora and fauna.

As the seasons turned, the townspeople continued their silent speculations about the enigmatic figure who graced their village. The Whisperer's presence had become a tapestry woven with whispered secrets and unspoken tales. They suspected him of possessing knowledge that transcended the limitations of mortal understanding, yet his voice remained an enigma to their ears.

In the end, it was the unspoken, the mysterious, and the unknown that captivated their imaginations. For in the realm of silence, the possibilities were endless, and the whispers of their suspicions echoed through their souls. And so, the Whisperer continued his ethereal journey, forever carrying the weight of their curiosity upon his enigmatic shoulders, forever veiled in the shroud of silence that had come to define him.

For it is in the realm of the unsaid that the greatest tales are born, where the power of imagination intertwines with the enigma of the unspoken. And as the townspeople returned to their daily lives, their whispered suspicions kept the legend of the Whisperer alive, a story that would endure long after the echoes of their footsteps had faded into the annals of time.

YOUR PINK SLIP INTACT

THE JUSTIFICATIONS FOR HOLDING YOUR OWN

In a realm where hearts danced to the rhythm of love, there lived a young couple named Lily and Ethan. Their bond was forged through the trials of life, a testament to the enduring strength of their connection. Their tale serves as a testament to the reasons that hold true in a profound relationship. Lily was a spirited and ambitious artist, while Ethan possessed a gentle soul and an unwavering determination. Together, they embarked on a journey through the tapestry of life, hand in hand, their dreams intertwining like vines in a secret garden. Their courting turned into now no longer without challenges. Storm clouds occasionally darkened their path, casting doubts and insecurities. But Lily and Ethan understood that relationships, like the seasons, must weather the storms to thrive. Trust, the bedrock upon which their love was built, held steadfast as their guiding light. They nurtured trust through open communication, sharing their deepest fears and vulnerabilities, fostering an environment of understanding and empathy. In the face of adversity, their unwavering trust fortified their bond, enabling them to weather any tempest that came their way.

Love, a delicate blossom, flourished between them. It was

not merely a fleeting emotion but a profound commitment, deep-rooted in their hearts. Their love was a tapestry woven with patience, compassion, and respect. Through the ebb and flow of life, they celebrated each other's victories and offered solace during moments of defeat.

Lily and Ethan knew that a successful relationship required more than love alone. They recognized the importance of individual growth and allowed each other the freedom to pursue their passions and dreams. They understood that personal fulfillment nurtured the relationship, creating an environment where two souls could soar while remaining grounded together.

In their journey, they discovered the art of compromise. They embraced the beauty of finding common ground, understanding that unity could be achieved through acceptance and empathy. They learned to listen to each other's voices, harmonizing their desires to create a symphony of shared goals and dreams.

Laughter and joy became the lifeblood of their relationship. In the midst of life's trials, Lily and Ethan found solace in laughter, playfulness, and shared adventures. They understood that life was a tapestry of both light and shadow and in their togetherness, they chose to embrace the light, savoring each moment of happiness and finding solace in the arms of one another during darker times.

As the years rolled by, Lily and Ethan's relationship deepened, their hearts entwined in a love that had stood the test of time. Their story serves as a reminder that in a profound relationship, trust, love, personal growth, compromise, and shared joy form the foundation on which two souls can build a lifetime of happiness.

And so, dear reader, may this tale illuminate the path to a fulfilling relationship, where hearts find solace, dreams take flight, and the reasons that hold true become the pillars of an enduring love story.

WHERE TO FIND NEW MENTAL STRENGTH

HOW TO GET THAT SPARK BACK

In a realm where hearts intertwined like the ivy on a moss-covered wall, there dwelled a couple named Seraphina and Oliver. Their love, like a timeless melody, had stood the test of time, but now they sought to rekindle the fires of mental challenge that had once burned bright.

Seraphina, a scholar with an insatiable thirst for knowledge, yearned to delve deeper into the realm of academia. Oliver, an adventurer at heart, sought to broaden his horizons beyond the familiar landscapes of their everyday lives. Together, they embarked on a quest to rejuvenate their intellectual connection, nurturing the seeds of curiosity that lay dormant within.

Guided by their shared yearning, they embarked on a journey of discovery. Seraphina buried herself in ancient tomes and scholarly works, unearthing forgotten wisdom and untold tales. She invited Oliver to partake in her intellectual endeavors, igniting lively conversations that stirred their minds and kindled a sense of wonder. In this exchange of ideas, they found a renewed mental challenge that breathed life into their relationship.

Oliver, in turn, sought solace in the beauty of nature. He wandered through untrodden paths, explored uncharted territories, and listened to the whispers of the wind. Seraphina, recognizing his newfound inspiration, joined him in his expeditions, allowing herself to be captivated by the wonders that surrounded them. Together, they marveled at the intricacies of the natural world, engaging in philosophical musings that expanded their horizons.

In their pursuit of intellectual rejuvenation, Seraphina and Oliver sought out diverse experiences. They attended lectures, engaged in lively debates, and immersed themselves in art and culture. They pushed the boundaries of their comfort zones, embracing the unfamiliar and the unknown. Through these shared experiences, they discovered the joy of intellectual exploration, expanding their understanding of the world and of each other.

Yet, they also cherished the importance of solitude in nurturing their individual growth. They encouraged one another to pursue personal passions, honoring the unique journeys that led them to self-discovery. Through this, they realized that the renewal of mental challenge within their relationship was an interplay of individual growth and shared intellectual pursuits.

As the seasons danced by, Seraphina and Oliver's renewed mental challenge breathed new life into their love. Their conversations grew richer, their minds intertwined like threads weaving a tapestry of shared intellect. They reveled in the beauty of expanding their knowledge together, finding solace in the fact that their relationship continued to evolve, just as they did as individuals.

Their journey stands as a testament to the transformative power of seeking intellectual stimulation within a relationship. Seraphina and Oliver discovered that the renewal of mental challenge was not a destination but a continuous journey, an ever-unfolding story that enriched their love.

And so, dear reader, may their tale inspire you to embark on your own quest for intellectual renewal within your relationship. Embrace the wonders of knowledge, nurture your individual passions, and invite your partner to join you in the exploration of ideas. In doing so, you shall discover a love that flourishes amidst the depths of intellectual curiosity, forever renewing and enriching your shared journey.

TAKE CHARGE OF YOUR EMOTIONS

In a world where emotions held sway over the hearts of mortals, there lived a young soul named Evangeline. Her spirit, though kind and gentle, often found itself overwhelmed by the tempestuous storms of feelings. Determined to gain mastery over her emotions, she embarked on a transformative journey.

Evangeline sought the wisdom of a venerable sage, a sage known for his deep understanding of the human psyche. With a heart filled with hope, she ventured to his secluded sanctuary nestled amidst ancient mountains. The sage greeted her with a knowing smile, recognizing the burning desire in her eyes.

He began to impart his wisdom, teaching her the art of self-awareness. Evangeline learned to recognize the subtle nuances of her emotions, to observe their ebb and flow without judgment. Through this mindful awareness, she gained insight into the inner workings of her heart and mind, understanding that emotions were merely passing waves upon the vast sea of her being.

The sage then introduced her to the power of breath, teaching her the art of deep and conscious breathing. As she inhaled the sweet fragrance of possibility and exhaled the burdens of negativity, she discovered a newfound sense of calm within. With each breath, she reclaimed her center, finding solace in the serenity that came from within.

Next, the sage revealed the secret of reframing thoughts. Evangeline learned to challenge the distorted narratives woven by her emotions, replacing them with more rational and compassionate perspectives. She understood that by reframing her thoughts, she could shift her emotional landscape, guiding her towards a state of balance and clarity.

As her lessons progressed, Evangeline delved into the realm of introspection. She explored the depths of her past, unearthing buried memories and unresolved traumas. With the sage as her guide, she embraced these experiences, acknowledging their existence without allowing them to define her present. In doing so, she liberated herself from the chains of the past, allowing her emotions to flow freely, yet guided by wisdom and understanding.

With time and practice, Evangeline discovered the power of intentional action. She learned to respond rather than react, to choose her words and deeds with deliberation and kindness. No longer a slave to the whims of her emotions, she wielded the reins of self-control, nurturing a sense of empowerment that permeated every aspect of her life.

As the seasons changed, Evangeline's transformation became evident to all who knew her. Her radiance shone like a beacon, drawing others towards her newfound serenity. With grace and empathy, she offered guidance to those who sought to gain control over their own emotions, sharing the wisdom she had acquired on her journey.

And so, dear reader, may Evangeline's tale inspire you to embark on your own quest for emotional mastery. Embrace self-awareness, harness the power of your breath, reframe your thoughts with compassion, and delve into the depths of introspection. Through intentional action and a steadfast commitment to growth, you shall discover the keys to gaining control of your emotions, unlocking a world of inner peace and strength.

THE UPDATED AND NEW BITCH

FOR WOMEN WHO ARE TOO NICE: THE SURVIVAL GUIDE

In a world brimming with vibrant colors and diverse souls, there once lived a young woman named Amelia. Her heart overflowed with kindness, and her gentle nature drew others to her like a soothing breeze on a summer's day. However, Amelia often found herself facing challenges as a result of her inherent niceness. Determined to navigate the complexities of life with grace and strength, she sought the guidance of a wise mentor who would unveil the survival guide for women who were too nice.

Amelia's journey led her to the dwelling of the venerable Elderia, a sage renowned for her wisdom and compassionate understanding. Elderia greeted Amelia with warmth, recognizing the struggles that accompanied a generous heart. With gentle eyes filled with knowledge, she began to impart the secrets of survival for women who exuded excessive kindness.

The first lesson Elderia shared with Amelia was the importance of self-care. She emphasized the significance of nourishing one's own well-being before extending kindness to others. Amelia learned to set healthy boundaries, recognizing that her own needs and happiness were just as important as those of others. By prioritizing self-care, she would fortify her spirit and retain the strength needed to navigate life's challenges.

The sage then revealed the art of assertiveness to Amelia. She taught her to communicate her needs and desires with clarity and confidence, without compromising her kindness. Amelia learned that assertiveness was not synonymous with aggression, but rather a tool for expressing herself authentically and ensuring her voice was heard. Through assertiveness, she would establish her presence, earning respect without sacrificing her innate kindness.

Next, Elderia guided Amelia in the practice of discernment. She encouraged her to trust her intuition and make choices that aligned with her values and beliefs. Amelia discovered that saying "no" when necessary was an act of self-preservation, allowing her to focus her energy on endeavors that truly resonated with her soul. In embracing discernment, she would shield herself from unnecessary burdens and preserve her emotional well-being.

Understanding the power of empathy within her, the sage unveiled the importance of selective compassion. Amelia learned that not every situation required her intervention or the expenditure of her emotional energy. By discerning when to extend her kindness and when to step back, she could maintain her compassionate nature without depleting herself. Selective compassion allowed her to make a meaningful impact where it truly mattered.

Lastly, Elderia shared the strength of building a support network. Amelia realized that she need not face life's challenges alone. She sought out like-minded individuals who valued kindness and understood her struggles. In their presence, she found solace and inspiration, knowing that she was not alone in her journey. The support network became her sanctuary, a place where she could find encouragement, advice, and the comfort of understanding hearts.

As the seasons passed, Amelia began to implement the survival guide for women who were too nice into her life. With each lesson learned and practiced, she grew in resilience and grace. The challenges that once overwhelmed her became stepping stones on her path to self-empowerment.

Amelia's story became an inspiration to women who shared her gentle nature. Her survival guide served as a beacon of hope, illuminating the path towards a balanced life where kindness and strength walked hand in hand. Her journey reminded others that kindness need not be a weakness but a wellspring of inner power.

And so, dear reader, may Amelia's tale empower you to embrace your inherent niceness while navigating life's complexities. Embrace self-care, practice assertiveness, cultivate discernment, exercise selective compassion, and seek the support of a nurturing network. In doing so, you shall embody the harmony of kindness and strength, forging a path of authenticity and resilience in this vast tapestry of life.

Notes

"Reasons Men Love Unrealistic Women" is a captivating fiction book that explores the complexities of relationships and societal expectations. Set in a modern world, the story delves into the lives of compelling characters and their entanglements with idealized versions of women. With its thought-provoking narrative and richly developed characters, the book challenges conventional notions of love, highlighting the allure and pitfalls of unrealistic expectations. This engrossing tale offers a deep exploration of human desires, vulnerability, and the search for meaningful connections in an imperfect world.